Satara

Enacting Code:
Zodiac

Solana

Solana

ALL RIGHTS RESERVED

An Honorable mention to my brother-in-law, William Cochran!

About Solana

<u>Radio</u> and <u>Television</u> Personality, Solana Psychic Energy Medium Healer, Reverend, Demonologist, Tantric Reiki Master (assisting in intimacy and sexual addictions) and Spiritual Guidance Counselor. Step into your knowing, with Solana Psychic energy medium and discover the world of synchronicity, while gaining coping tools and activating your inner GPS.

Since the tender age of six Psychic Energy Medium Solana has been a witness to the "living dead." Her abilities from that moment on were transformed by daily paranormal occurrences and an ever-increasing talent to see the "Energy" that surrounds both the living and the Dead, and in time was able to discern how to heal people through maneuvering the Chakra System.

Naturally, Solana's path led to a life study of the supernatural, and she now teaches Certified courses in psychic abilities, mediumship and how to see and read auras.

Solana hosts on Youtube and co-hosts on SOC Radio, BTR Radio, on World Views, Metaphysical Topics and the paranormal as well as offering her own services for ghost clearing, investigating, energy work, channeling and mediumship. Solana has assisted people worldwide in moving past fear, leading the way to understand and healing for themselves, their relationships and careers.

As a fearless Demonologist, she joins forces with her Guides and Ascended Masters, completing an incredible group who battle relentlessly against dark energies and otherworldly trouble makers nationwide. During these harrowing encounters most would be terrified- but for irrepressible Solana, it's part of her soul purpose and a challenge she welcomes. Solana has experienced everywhere she goes, even on vacations! This Series found one of her experiences worthy of a 20-minute spot on, My Haunted Vacation, although edited, an experience none the less, you can view it here, https://www.youtube.com/watch?v=yUSmJXKhABs

Also an avid Hemp Activist, Solana seeks truth in all things with keen integrity to bring solutions in restoring peace and balance to our world. Industrial CBD-rich Hemp products.

As an Author, you can find Solana stories, My Paranormal Life, A Monthly Series of my true Paranormal Experiences, at, www.bellesprit.com under the Paranormal section.

Solana has assisted people all over the world to move past their fears, giving way to understanding, for themselves, their relationships and careers.

Solana encourages us all to repeat daily, "I AM connected, grounded, balanced, protected and flowing in the Love of the Divine."

Please visit, www.psychicsolana.wix.com/services and Order Your Experience Today.

Revelation Chapter 3:14

"And unto the angel of the Church of the La-od-i-ce'and write: These things saith the Amen, the faithful and true witness the beginning of the creation of God."

The name of the truthful son of God is, A'men,' pronounced, (Aah-mon'), having been cloned 17 times at the point of the New World (Earth).

Table of Contents:

Chapter One

Snow in July

As the snow began to fall, it took everyone by surprise!

It was late July, and the snow never fell at this "hottest time of the year," people pulled their cars over and watched from within the buildings and homes throughout the coastal towns and cities to get a better look at the phenomenon.

The sky was full of grey, pink and white clouds, rolling over the earth, with blinding white snow falling from its belly, leaving everything in its path covered in the thick white powder.

Children playing in their own backyards began gasping for air and falling to the ground. A mother runs to her son who lays helpless under the swing set, holding his neck with both hands. His tongue is hanging to the side of his open mouth, and as he struggles to breathe, he suddenly releases his grip and dies in his mother's arms.

While she is weeping for her loss, she becomes overwhelmed by the gases. Gripping her son in one arm and fighting for her last breath, she tries to get them both back into the safety of her home. Just a few steps from the back porch, she collapses and loses her battle falling to her death with her son still clutched in her arms.

Whatever was happening during this freak storm, was affecting everyone who was outside. Some people started to venture out of their homes to get a better look at the falling snow. What they witnessed was the shocking reality that countless others of their neighbors who were unfortunate to be outside when this storm came, were dead or dying - falling to the ground as they struggled to reach safety.

Teenagers and students of all ages, returning home from after-school activities fell victim to the deadly snow. Fear rose in the masses as more and more bodies began to litter the streets and walkways of every grid in the path of the unrelenting cloud.

Just as one man was about to open his front door, he heard the familiar siren sound effect that signals the beginning of an emergency broadcast.

"This is an Emergency, this is an Emergency, repeated the announcer. This is the activation of the emergency broadcast system, for the eastern states, this information is for all within the sound of this broadcast. Stay in your homes and places of enclosed shelter, do not venture outdoors, civil authorities in your area have reported a massive storm, traveling west from the Atlantic Ocean, moving north/east, they are tracking the storm and asking everyone stay inside for safety. There have been reports that this storm carries a deadly snow, we are receiving reports of countless fatalities and injuries with more expected as this storm makes its way across the east coast. All those within the sound of this alert are to remain where they are until further notice. We will update you as more information comes through. Stay inside your homes and places of safety, a deadly snow has fallen across part of the East coast."

Radio stations began broadcasting the same warnings. People traveling in their cars were to turn off all ventilation systems and return all domes to the covered positions. They were to return to their homes and remain there until further notice. The snow looked like snow but did not leave the air cold.

Several people that thought it was safe to exit their cars began to choke as if they were being poisoned. People started falling to the ground, dying within minutes. Those that stayed inside, undercover, watched in horror as the snow began to melt, just as quickly as the deadly precipitation fell. Unable to bear the thought of living, some people upon witnessing the death of their loved ones, ran outside knowing they too would perish.

Dogs stood guard over their owner's bodies, as their leashes were caught in the grips of the dying people. Other dogs and cats were running loose, escaping through open doors and the clutches of those falling victim to the weather phenomena. Those left watching in horror from their homes noticed that the snow was not affecting the cats and dogs.

A mother helplessly watched from the front window of her home as her daughter struggled to pull herself up the walkway. With arms reached out, pleading for her mother's help, she collapsed and died just a few feet from the front door.

Two men tried to rescue a couple of guys who were near their car. When they reached the dying men, they attempted to carry them to safety. While they were not concerned for themselves, they too began to choke and find it harder to breathe. As they tried to pick up the dying men, they also became casualties of the devastating event.

Chapter Two

Evacuation

Diane was horrified as she watched these events from her car, but she did not dare to get out to help others, in fear for her own life. She obeyed the emergency broadcasts and turned off her air conditioner, while she remained safely inside her vehicle.

Overwhelmed with concern, her priority is to get herself and her children, to the Lab where her husband works. Adding to the urgency of this thought, she begins hearing John's voice within her mind, summoning her to the lab.

The drive home is like an obstacle course as she has to dodge abandoned cars and bodies lying everywhere. Just a few blocks from her dwelling, she notices the clouds moving over her neighborhood.

Diane is fearful for the rest of her family, as she wonders where they are. Are they caught in this deadly snow or safe at home? She has already lost several female friends and members of her family due to a virus that has, to this day, remained untreatable.

As she turns into her neighborhood, she notices one of the neighbor's robots running out to assist its owner. The man who the robot is trying to help is halfway out of his car when he grabs his throat and begins choking.

The robot assists him out of the car and into the house where the man dies in the doorway. Just like the cats and dogs, the snow did not affect the robots.

The Robots were designed to look like human beings except that they were an off-white color, a mixture of grey and white. They wear grey uniforms well-suited to their position. They can think and resolve situations with common sense and compassion. They are unable to cause any harm to themselves, any human being or any other living animal.

Robots serve many useful purposes in this society. They assist in domestic household services including housekeeping, childcare and overall safety and security of the home and its occupants. They also have replaced humans in what used to be employment positions of a service nature such as clerks, servers in restaurants, and other menial jobs.

"Phone, call home," Diane thought with her mind. Ginny, her 17-year-old daughter, answered, "Hello!" "Ginny, this is my mom."

"Hey, mom, where are you at?"

"I am on my way home. Is it snowing there?"

"Yes! It just started, isn't that weird!" Ginny said In a panicked voice.

"Don't go outside! I'll be home in 2 minutes. Is your brother home?" Tommy, her 15-year-old son, had football practice after school.

"Yes! He got home before it started snowing." Relieved, Diane told Ginny to pack up the emergency bags, they had to get to the Lab where her husband John works.

"Don't forget the bag in the safe, looks like we are going to need that sooner than planned!" Directed Diane.

"What about the Robot and the pets?" Ginny asked.

"We will have to leave them for now. Your father has the only pet we need to worry about at the Lab. He took it this morning in preparation for the transfer. I am pulling up the driveway now."

Safely inside the garage, Diane closes the door and turns on the automatic hot air blowers for the car. Once the snow melts from the exterior of the vehicle and the garage floor, she gets out and heads for the entry into the house.

Hurried now, she inspects the bags Ginny left on the kitchen table and looks to make sure everything is in order. Tommy is the first one down the stairs as Diane begins calling for her children to come quickly.

"Tommy, did you put the pets in their safe room?" Diane asks as Tommy leaps down the stairs.

"Yes, mom! I put them up with plenty of food and water, and I hooked up the Robot in its carrier, so it is ready to go!" He knew that was the next question. Ginny follows behind him, carrying the bag from the safe.

"Good! Everything is here, let's go! I will call your father when we get into the car." Diane said as they head back out to the garage.

After putting the bags into the trunk, Tommy and Ginny jump into the car before the garage door opens.

"Phone, call John," Diane said as they back out of the garage. John answers on the first ring, knowing it's Diane, he says, "Diane, get to the lab as soon as possible!"

"We are on our way; did you see the cause of the snow?" Diane asks, praying he has the answer.

"Yes! You will not believe what I found! Just hurry up and get here. Do not get out of the car until you arrive, and drive with all the vents closed. Do not even run the air conditioner!

You can come in the back entrance, come all the way to the doors in the underground parking." He says with urgency in his voice.

"Alright, we will see you in about 20 minutes. I love you!" She says in her most courageous tone.

"I love you too! Call me when you have arrived." John says bravely.

As they start to drive down the street, they notice several of their neighbors lying dead beside their vehicles. Some of them are alone, while others have members of their families stacked on top of them; apparently, they too had tried to help them and died right there with them.

One woman runs out of her house as Diane's car passes by, she begins to cry for help as she sees her husband lying next to his car. Diane wants to stop and help her but knows there is nothing she can do for her. They also notice cats and dogs running around, not affected at all by the snow.

"I feel so bad for those poor people!" Ginny says with tears in her eyes.

"I know sweetie, me too! Strange it isn't affecting the animals." Was all Diane could express.

When they are out of their neighborhood, Diane puts the vehicle in Fly mode; they lift up into the air and proceed to the lab.

Chapter Three

John and Diane

John and Diane met at the Birthday Party of a mutual friend, while attending the New York City Medical College, in the year 10,142. They were both from small families with only one sibling each.

Diane, being the younger of two sisters, was from Houston, Texas. Her father was a Doctor of Veterinary Medicine, and her mother was a Science Teacher at one of the local High Schools.

Her elder sister was also a Teacher of Health; she taught Physical Education and was the Volleyball Coach for a High School in Florida.

John was from a little town in the mountains of Arizona.

His parents were both family doctors, they ran the only doctor's office for 200 miles, in their small town of Payson.

Just like Diane, John had an older sister who did not follow the path of their parents. She had decided early on that she wanted to be a Professional Actor/Dancer. She was living in New York City performing on Broadway. John was going to be a great scientist.

At the age of 28, he had devoted his life to the Study of Internal Medicine, Infectious Diseases, with an Understudy in General and Cardiothoracic Surgery.

Diane was equally as brilliant, at the age of 26, she had decided on specializing in Obstetrics/Gynecology, with an Understudy in Family Medicine.

At the time Diane was about to start her Internship at Holy Grace Hospital in New Jersey, John was close to completing his studies and had already begun looking for a place to begin his research.

When they first met, they talked all night, about everything they wanted to do once they were finished with med school. The night swept away so fast, they were almost late for class the next morning. Diane knew as soon as John left that she was going to marry that man!

John had a similar feeling but did not want to rush anything. He was very committed to his education and rarely dated. He was a very handsome man, 6' tall, with brownish blond hair, and deep blue eyes. He was almost too skinny because he did not eat right and was always studying, so he did not get much exercise. Very headstrong, he knew what he was destined to do in this life.

The family was always in the back of his mind as a second priority behind getting his career started. Now he had to think twice about that.

Diane was a beautiful woman with a personality to match, with long brown hair, brown eyes, and a smile that would calm all your fears.

Standing at 5 foot 6 inches with a beautiful full figure, she was a bold, strong woman but very compassionate about her choice of career. She knew from a young age that she wanted to be a Doctor.

While she understood that God had a bigger plan for those she could not help, she would heal all those within her powers! She was ready to start her new life as a Doctor as well as a Doctor's wife!

It was during John's last week of college that he learned he was accepted at the world's largest Research and Development for

Scientific Advancements (R.D.S.A.), located in Seattle Washington, in which he was the last Intern taken on that year. He was extremely excited, even though it meant moving away from Diane.

He walked up to her apartment, pondering how he was going to tell her his good news. He had mentioned his application for the post to her just after they had met. Indeed, she would have remembered that part of the conversation!

Although they had become closer than either of them thought possible at the time. She may not be thrilled for me, was his thought as he walked in front of her apartment door.

While he knocked on her door, he thought he would just be out with it the minute he saw her!

The moment she opened the door, he threw his arms around her, while lifting her up and swinging her around, he blurted out,

"I got the post at the R.D.S.A.! Is that not the most exciting news?" he threw that in for extra excitability factors!

Her response was full of admiration for him!

"That's wonderful John! I am so happy for you! I know what this must mean to you!" Being caught up in his excitement, she continued his embrace with a tight hug and the sweetest kiss he had ever received from her!

He became extremely excited feeling her body so close to his.

Her lips on his lips, they both felt the spark of energy that was now consuming them both.

He started kissing her neck, "I love you so much, Diane! I love you, I love you, I love you!" He repeated while moving his hands up her waist, feeling her body respond, he slid his hand over her breast and pulled her closer to him.

Diane felt his hard body as she pressed up against him. She began to feel the pulsating heat from between her legs, rising up into her stomach. As John started caressing her breast, Diane felt her body begin to move back and forth against John's hard, hot body.

In between kisses, she expressed her love for him.

"I love you too!" as she moved her lips from his, she started kissing him on his neck, back to his lips never leaving his flesh, "I love you too John!" She could feel her excitement running through her body, "John wait, we have to stop!

You know I love you and want to make love to you more than anything right now but, we both know that I am committed to staying a virgin until I am married!" The words spilled out of her mouth most lovingly.

Still embracing her, John conceded that he understood. "You are right! I know we were just caught up in the excitement!" As he pressed his body against her body, he looked her straight in the eyes; he uttered the words she had longed to hear.

"Will you marry me, Diane?" Without even thinking about it, she squeezed him tighter and answered with a resounding, "YES! I will marry you!".

He surprised her when he suggested they go out right away and purchase an engagement ring.

"Let's go out and celebrate!" he added. "I want you to put on your prettiest outfit. I will meet you back here in 30 minutes." After kissing her goodbye, he went to the door, turned around and looked at her and said, "Don't worry about the details for this evening; I will take care of everything!"

"I will be waiting for you! Now hurry and go so that I can get ready." She smiled at him as he went out the door.

Exactly 30 minutes later, John was knocking on Diane's apartment door. "Come in!" Diane yelled from her bedroom. She came walking out just as he closed the door.

"WOW! You look beautiful!" He stammered, unable to think of anything else to say. Who could imagine with such a wonderfully, beautiful woman standing in front of them?

"You like." She said shyly. "I like very much!" He said as he kissed her on her cheek. She was dressed in a low cut, form-fitting dress, made of Blue satin, his favorite color. Her hair was down, in long curls that flowed down onto her shoulders. He put her arm in his, and they headed out the door towards his car.

"So, what have you planned for this evening? She asked, as he opened the door for her and assisted her inside. In a soft, mysterious voice, he replied, "You will see!"

Diane watched him as he went to the front of the car until he sat down beside her. How handsome he looked in his Dark Blue Suit!

"That suit really brings out the blue in your eyes. You look very handsome tonight; we must be going to an extraordinary place." Fishing once again for any insight into the plans he made for them.

"Flattery will get you nowhere. I am not telling you!" He said playfully as he started the car.

As they pulled up in front of Styles Jewels, the most prestige's jeweler in town. John looked over at Diane and said, "This is our first stop, to the first steps of our new life together."

Taking her hands into his, he kissed both hands,

"Wait right there, and allow me to assist you out of the car."

Without waiting for a reply, John got out of the car and walked around to Diane's door. As he opened the door, he held out his hand. Diane took his hand and allowed him to assist her out of the car. "Thank You, Kind Sir."

"You're most welcomed ma' lady" when they walked up to the Jewelry Store door, the manager meets them in expectation of their arrival.

"Good evening Mr. Styles, thank you for staying open for us," John spoke as if he had already spoken to this man. "Good evening sir, miss. It is my pleasure to be of service to you. I have everything ready for you. Right, this way." Mr. Styles instructed.

As they stepped up to the long jewelry case, Mr. Styles was unlocking the small sliding door. He then presented a tray that contained several rows of beautiful engagement rings. "I took the liberty to present these choices for you to select from."

He then began to explain to the couple the quality of Diamond each ring held, holding each piece up as he went from one beautiful ring to the next.

They were all so beautiful, Diane had a hard time choosing between them. She was able to narrow it down to two rings that were about the same size.

One was a 2k-marquise diamond and the other a 2-1/2k-teardrop diamond. The 2k rock was fit for a size 7 finger, and the 2 1/2 k diamond ring was sized for an eight.

Diane being a size 7, decided to take the 2k diamond so that she could take it with her tonight.

"Shall I wrap this for you?" Mr. Styles offered. "No, thank you, I will be putting this on her finger right away!" As he placed the ring on her finger, John once again asked her to be his wife.

"Will you accept this ring and become my wife?" Smiling that mesmerizing smile, Diane agreed by saying "For the rest of my life!"

After paying for the ring, they walked out of the Jewelry Store and headed down the street.

"Where are you taking me now?" John just kept walking without saying a word, just a smile on his face.

Just down a few doors down from the store was a little Italian restaurant.

"Here we are," John announced, arriving at the location where they had their first official date.

"Oh, how wonderful for you to have chosen this restaurant for our celebration. It is my favorite place, you know." Diane proclaimed in recognition of the Italian restaurant being the place of their first date. As they entered the restaurant, the owner came running over to them.

"Ah, hello Mr. John, Miss Diane welcome, welcome, we have your table ready for you, please come with me. I have the bottle of wine you requested all ready for you at the table. Your Escargot will be out momentarily. Please, sit back, relax, and enjoy! Allow me to pour you both some wine. I would also like to extend my congratulations to you both on your engagement!" he rattled on as he began to bow while turning away from them.

"Allow me to make a toast. To my dearest darling Diane, thank you for agreeing to be my wife, my life mate, my love. May every day be filled with your smile."

The two wine glasses chimed together leaving a ringing in the air as they sipped from their glasses, in encircled arms.

"This is the beginning of a beautiful new chapter in our lives!" John continued.

"I second that! And congratulations on your new post!" Diane said with a smile as she raised her glass up, then after taking another drink, she set it back down on the table.

She then leaned into John and whispered in his ear, "I feel very blessed to have you in my life, and I would like to thank you for making this a memorable evening for me. I will cherish this moment for the rest of my days."

She then kissed him on his lips so gently, holding his face softly within her hands, it felt more like a smooth feather slowly going over his mouth, and he felt a rush of electricity as their lips came together, he felt it all the way down to his soul.

He could tell that she felt it as well. She let out a little moan at the exact time he felt the rush. If that kiss had lasted another second longer he might have forgotten they were in a public place and taken her right there and then!

They both realized what had just happened and held each other for a brief moment as if to acknowledge the energy they were feeling.

With a smile, Diane said, "I love you, John Lott!" John gazed into her eyes and replied, "I love you, Diane Lott!"

Their waiter interrupted them setting the first of many delectable dishes onto the table. Over one scrumptious course after the other, they had determined that a spring wedding would be most appropriate for their working schedules. It would have to wait until next year because they wanted to have enough time to plan for an extended honeymoon. They agreed on a small wedding with mainly family and a few close friends attending.

Money was not going to be an issue for them theirs was time. Time spent away from their newly appointed positions was going to have to be done in a creative yet beneficial manner. It was going to mean many extra hours for the first year. They finished their dinner and decided to end the evening stargazing from the rooftop of Diane's apartment.

Med school was just 3 weeks away from ending. They spent all their spare time helping each other box up and pack for the move. While waiting for the Moving Company to load their belongings onto the transporter. They worked out all the visitation trips that would take place. It was a 1/2-hour flight from New Jersey to Seattle. They would take turns making the trip.

Chapter Four

Future World

Being told of their lineage, who Created them (cloned from the original 7 beings, Michael, Raphael, Daniel, Ezekiel, Malachi, Ariel, and Gabriel), and they from the Amen, the first manifestation of God.

They were from the Planet Orabus, in the Orion Galaxy. They knew of **their capabilities, manifesting all 10 senses; sight, hearing, taste, touch,** telepathic, telepathy, telekinesis, seeing energy, emotions and free will. Satara was the 3rd settlement since Orabus.

Their technologies gave flight to a simple life, with every household able to obtain every convenience.

Space travel, Flying Automobiles (capable of transforming into aquatic and rover vehicles, with just a thought), Robots (doing all the necessary yet civil servant positions, domestic, janitorial, waste management, machinery, and the like) Voice Recognition Homes/Appliances/Food Replicators, Automated Physicians and Dentist, Communities in the sky and within the planet. Weather control (maintaining 4 mild seasons).

Peace reigned for many years until the resources started to run out and civil unrest caused riots and a rise in crime. Then the war broke out, and the destruction of the females was suddenly revealed.

Satara was a beautiful planet, with green lands and blue oceans. The world around them consisted of flying vehicles, sized to accommodate individuals, families, and businesses. Cargoes were transported in underground tunnels and teleportation chambers. Within the cities, buildings operated businesses on the first five levels, with housing underneath and above.

They were all built with transporters that ran above, underneath and into the Inner Earth Cities. Each transporter was designed with the purpose and need of the products it would carry.

Made of thin, durable metal, metallic in color it was resistant to all types of conditions. All were equipped with temperature controlled cars and entertainment for each passenger.

The tunnels ran along a grid under the earth as well as above the ground. Giving way to the outer earth for the development of the Ecosystems and environmentally safe housing.

Housing was available above the earth in the form of Sky Homes. Multi-leveled structures that contained 50 to 100 apartments. Sky homes were positioned on the border of the cities. Levitation was possible for those living in the Sky Homes.

Placed at 4000 feet above the earth, powered by solar hovering squid, they were the answer to the dwindling availability of land. The squid got its name because it looks like a large squid, eight legs spread out to adjustable lengths, each leg contains energy provided by the solar panel connected to the end of the squid. The solar gives energy to the hovering disk that enables the building to remain stationary.

Interplanetary travel was available to all citizens. Vacations, retreats, could take place on neighboring planets. Public transportation consisted of Personal Transporters, Teleportation Chambers, and a High-Speed Rail system, that ran above and below ground.

Satara's Scientist had made such strides as too can Clone a

variety of Robot species, to assist in daily necessities, such as Housekeepers, Groundskeepers, Medical Assistance in Nurses, Doctors, Police Officers and Custodial Personnel, were all replaced by the more durable, everlasting biogenetically engineered entities.

The Biogen robots were created to take over the personal and public duties, made to look like a human being, the Biogen's stayed with a Family for over 100 years before getting upgraded or replaced. Needing little to no maintenance, the Biogen Robots proved to be useful in many positions of menial tasks.

Such tasks also included running both the Hydro-Electric Plants and the Weather System, the Biogen Robots monitored and maintained the 200 stations, strategically placed around the planet.

These stations enabled electricity at minimal cost and the Seasons to remain mild while providing stable water levels, preventing flooding, drought, tornadoes, hurricanes, blizzards and other natural disastrous weather conditions.

Scientists were dumbfounded when fish started showing up on the shores of southern beaches, as they felt they were doing everything they could to preserve the planet for future generations.

Evidence was found that the Earth's Core was heating up and caused riverbeds and oceans to boil the sea life. Underground volcanoes began to erupt on a massive scale.

During their research, they found new bacteria beginning to develop due to the rise in temperature of the world's water reserve. This brought their attention to the Earth's changes. Evidence of the planet's rotation was revealed once core and carbon samples were taken and applied to the information about the depletion of the natural resources. Bringing to light the shift that happens every 25,000 years.

Gradual at first, taking 5 years to complete, the earth's inner layers tell a tale of axles shifting from North to South in the final lasting only hours.

Astronomers took the task of researching these changes to the path of planets in our solar system, going back 25,000 years, it was discovered that a particular alignment with 2 of the outer planets traveling within the constellation above Satara, could change the gravitational pull of the earth, causing it to shift its poles.

It was thought to be the alignment of planets that brought on these earth changes, that man had clearly survived, so it was labeled a natural occurrence, given a low threat level and told not investigated any further.

These times would prove to be a challenging enough for the scientist as recent viruses and diseases became more and more resilient to their methods of treatments. Men and women were becoming sterile, unable to conceive or many miscarrying. Women were dying at an alarming rate, due to untreatable cancer and viruses.

Chapter Five

Destiny

John spent their last night together over at Diane's apartment. The time went quickly, just as it did the first night spent engrossed in conversation. They stayed awake all night. When the morning sun came into view, they kissed and embraced, then they got into their own cars and flew up into the air in opposite directions.

The first few months went by quickly. Plans for their wedding began, they were to be married in a lavish garden with family and a few friends around them.

They choose to live in Seattle, where John could continue his research. Diane was able to start her own practice and settled into her new life with John.

Once their union was official and a glorious week spent together, the dedicated couple returned to their work.

Married for 4 years, they gave birth to a daughter named Ginny. Born March 8th, 10,147. Two years later, their son Tommy was born. He was born March 24th.

Their lives were stapled in traditions of the past; however, the technology of the day afforded the average household the most of every modern convenience.

Underground homes where available to those who wished to live within the earth and Sky-homes became popular within the last 30 years.

John and Diane bought a big four bedroom home, just outside of the city. Finding a home that was a short drive to work for them both helped in the decision to purchase in a traditional location. Traditional only in the manner of the construction and location. The house was fully operational with the latest lighting, appliances, home theater screens in every room including the kitchen, bedrooms and game room, with surround sound wired in the walls.

The garage had an air dryer built into the floor and could store several vehicles.

Knowing that they would only be having 2 children, they had decorated two of the bedrooms, one for a girl, the other for a boy. Both rooms reflected the sex of the child, pink and yellows for their baby girl, and blue and greens for a little boy. With scenery walls that changed with the seasons.

A crib that grew with the child, starting as a bassinet and ending as a full-size bed. It was considered to be an excellent area to start a family and raise their children.

John felt secure enough to devote most of his time to his research. He understood the importance of his work, as it meant a better future for all mankind.

Chapter Six

Changing Times

The past several months had been unusually hard on the earth and its inhabitants. Hurricanes, tornadoes, floods, snowstorms, volcanic eruptions, and earthquakes seem to be at an all-time high. Increasing in strength and intensity, these storms have been wiping out entire coastline cities and causing destruction up to 250 miles of land.

Hurricanes 400 miles wide with 300 miles per hour winds, destroying everything within its path, one right after the other giving no time to search for the living or the dead before striking yet another hard blow.

Areas never touched by the horrifying winds, were now experiencing category 5 tornadoes. Entire communities were flattened, as the death tolls were rising.

Tropical storms reaching the areas unaffected by the Ocean's fury, flooding rivers and lakes, streams becoming oceans, sweeping away all that lay in its path.

Leaving nothing but destruction affected by the wrath of the waters. Volcanoes around the earth that had been dormant for generations, now pouring out their fiery judgment onto the earth's surface.

Killing all within its grasp, leaving ashes in its wake, lasting for days, the fiery red lava was determined in its destiny of destruction. Earthquakes shifting the earth's core, swallowing all that inhabit its soil. Leaving structures, highways, homes, businesses, torn from their foundations and pulled into the earth's gaping holes. Piles of rubble left with tops of buildings bulging out.

As if, a bomb had gone off from underneath the surface of the earth. Causing Tidal waves, forcing water to engulf islands with millions of human beings swept away with the water currants, returning to the deep waters with its catch.

Snowstorms that stranded travelers within 10 feet of snow. While pulling others off the sides of mountains in its thunderous rolling wave. Separating loved ones, denying the sick and elderly the assistance needed for their survival.

Animals, insects, and livestock of all kinds buried underneath the freezing tomb. These were natural weather conditions that are necessary to maintain the flow of life, however; these were events that were becoming a threat to that life. Many Scientist and Meteorologist, had been alerted by the recent activities of the earth and began their investigation into the cause of the anomaly. Having been aware of the research going on over at the R.D.S.A., they wondered if these weather patterns were connected to the experiments being conducted.

Joining forces with the team of scientists was the only solution for the R.D.S.A., they were devising a plan and would need more assistance if they were to finish in time.

Scientists and doctors were dealing with viruses and diseases that remained mysterious as to their origins. Flesh-eating bacteria spread as did leprosy and other immunological disorders, affecting the immune system. Women were becoming barren, unable to conceive and dying at alarming rates, due to cancers in the reproductive system.

Men and women alike, would suddenly snap, and execute plans to kill randomly, as well as murder their children and other family members.

If the perpetrators survived, they would have no acceptable reasoning for taking the lives of their children or loved ones. They would give excuses like, "I didn't like the way the children spoke to me," or "voices in my head told me my child was evil and had to be destroyed."

Unwarranted wars were breaking out, killing became a payday for those in charge of these wars. Greed and power were the next obtainable status, creating rifts in the psyche of the people.

Relationships became increasingly tricky, thoughts and feelings were harder to read. The once mutual respect and dignity seemed unbalanced. People were less tolerant of each other, driving the Divorce rates up as well as the suicidal casualties.

The technology was everywhere, voice command computers were as small as a fingernail and could be broadcast in 3D and on any size screen or wall. Giving distractions to take the place of interaction, making everyone feel separated, disconnecting from each other.

Everyday life seemed to be unraveling, and no one understands what was happening to them.

Chapter Seven

A World Aware of Time

As Diane began her descent down onto the bridge, which leads to the Industrial Parkway, her thoughts were running in so many directions, she nearly hit a body that was lying near the side of the road.

"Mom, look out!" Diane heard the words from her daughter just as she jerked the car into the left lane. Missing the man's body by inches.

"Oh my God mom, look at all the people, there are so many of them." Shaking and crying, Ginny put her hands up to her face, covering her eyes from these horrific visions, sobbing between her words,

"Hurry up mom, get us to the lab, hurry up mom, get us to the lab, hurry…" sobbing repeatedly.

Diane could not reply. She was not able to speak any comforting words to her daughter. She could not do anything but look straight ahead. Dodging abandoned cars and lifeless bodies randomly spread out over the road.

Tommy sat motionless in the back seat of the car. His mind is not able to register what his eyes were witnessing. Their car turned down the street toward the lab. Diane noticed several dogs running around. Her thoughts went back to a time John had been doing some experiments concerning the discovery of an unusual gene found in the canine DNA.

"Why would that have such an effect on the dog's apparent immunity to this deadly snow?" Her expression must have conveyed her confusion, as her daughter asked, "Are you worried we won't make it safely to the lab mom?"

Snapping back into her current situation, Diane stuttered, "What, oh no honey, I'm sure your father has taken every precaution to make sure we arrive unharmed. I was just thinking about the dogs again." Putting her hand on her daughter's knee and giving a little squeeze, she added, "I know we will be safe once inside the tunnel."

"Phone, call John," Diane said as she pulled the car into the parking lot of the lab.

"Are you here?" Answered John.

"Yes, we are pulling in front of the gate to the tunnel now," responded Diane.

"Alright, I'm opening the gate now, drive back to the last door, stay in the car, I will meet you there," John instructed.

"OK, see you inside." Diane moved the car down the long tunnel. The lab was underground, in a building that was designed in two parts.

The top 3 levels were above ground, and the lower three levels were underground. The tunnel brings you through three vertical, thick steel doors. As she drove through the second door, Diane felt the absence of any air.

Once the third thick paneled door closed behind her, she entered the parking level for the lower building. Armed, masked guards waved her through the entrance, motioning her to drive down to the back of the parking garage.

While slowly driving, Diane noticed that there were a lot more cars than usual. Driving all the way to the back door, as instructed, Diane pulled into the spot closest to the entrance. They waited in the car until John arrived. While waiting for John, Diane's memories of John's new position came flooding into her mind.

John had been so excited to learn of his new post because he had been waiting years to begin the research needed for the survival of his race. Their advances in technologies gave them the ability to determine exactly how long their current resources would last. The research he would be involved with concerned the development of a New Planet.

A scientist by the name of Nostradamus, in the year 10,105 discovered information about the depletion of Sataras resources. From his research, he found that the earth was over 6 trillion years old. Oil, natural gas, the land's ability to recover from generations of use was coming to an end. Nostradamus was able to determine that the planet's resources would be gone by the year 10,120 by their calendar.

Nostradamus also predicted that the planet would self-destruct by way of earthquakes, volcanic eruptions, and flooding, all fatal catastrophes. As the planet's evidence showed, it had gone through at least 4 times already.

Their only hope for survival would be to leave Satara before everything on it was destroyed. This begun the formation of the secret society within the R.D.S.A. What John didn't know, was that only one percent of the Sataras population were to be included in their plans of evacuation. The discovery of the planet's shifting its poles and the fact the natural resources were running out, meant that they would have to execute a plan to leave most of the earth's inhabitants behind.

Along with the insights of manipulating DNA, they were able to develop the blueprint for creating planets. Scouts were sent out into the Galaxy to search for the right conditions for such an endeavor.

Teams of scientist were grouped together for the designs of this new Star system. One group would be responsible for the planet's inner layers, another would be in charge of the outer layers and the atmosphere needed for life. There was a team for the Horticulture, one for the mammals and sea life.

A team that called themselves the Noah Group was responsible for all the livestock that was to live on the surface. The development of the New World depended on all these teams to work together.

They worked diligently, using every technology available. The search for a new home took on a life of its own. Understanding the most basic assembly of all plants, fish, and mammals, they were able to recreate all needed elements of life. Reproduction of the planet was now ready to take place. The scouts returned to the location of another pocket in space that seemed compatible with the elements needed to produce the right atmospheric conditions for the Creation of a Planet. In which oxygen and water would thrive.

The two teams responsible for the inner and outer layers set out to the location and begun the process for the planet system. The elements were placed in the gel canisters and shot out into the atmosphere. The first chemical reaction was the production of gases that melded together forming a circular formation with the atoms introduced from the other canister. In a spinning motion, the atoms from the planet while combining with the gases in the atmosphere a new system is created.

While the planet was being created, the spiraling atoms detached from the others and went out into the atmosphere forming 3 planets, surrounding the main world, providing the needed gravity to support the new planets in the star system.

The next step was to bring water to the planet. Using a large amount of ice brought in motherships, 3 huge balls of ice were simply dropped onto the surface of the New World. The pressure from the frozen waters fall produced a layer of earth to fly up into the air; particles crashing into each other caused the formation of the moon.

The moon provided the last step in the gravitational pull, needed for maintaining gravity on the earth. Hitting the planet with such force, the frozen water melting just after impact then formed large and small pools of water. Giving way to oceans and flowing canals and rivers that carried water inland.

This project had been in the advanced stages when John began participating in the development of the livestock. His work included the new development of DNA and changing of the DNA in animals. Which is how John found the unusual gene in the canine DNA.

Chapter Eight

Discovering Intentions of A. I.

Knock, knock, Diane was startled back into reality by the sharp clanging she felt from the driver's side window. She screamed as she looked into the face of a masked man motioning her to roll down the window. When she saw his white coat, she relaxed knowing it was John.

"Diane, slowly open the window. Just enough to grab these masks. Everyone put one on and then get out of the car. Go directly to the door and go inside the hallway." He was speaking in a calm but hurried voice.

Without question, the three of them put the mask over their faces and exited the car. All three of them ran straight to the entrance and into the hallway. After grabbing the bags from the trunk, John followed them inside the door and locked it.

"Don't remove your mask until we are inside the Lab, don't look at or talk to anyone, look straight ahead and follow me" Diane grabbed John's hand and held it tight as they began to walk to the lab, followed by 2 armed guards.

"What's going on here John? Why all the security? Who do all those cars belong to?"

"I will answer all your questions once we are securely in the lab," he put his arm around her and pulled her close enough to hear him whisper.

"They are watching and can hear us" They silently walked down the deserted hallway, as they walked by a door that signs read, **Authorized Personnel Only**.

The door opened, and Diane heard voices yelling, arguing from inside. When she looked to see who was screaming, it was a man that looked like the President of the United States. Diane looked at John, who was looking straight ahead and just pulled Diane along as if to say, don't ask.

Once inside the Lab, the two-armed guards stood just outside the closed door. John set the bags on the table and removed his mask. "You can all remove your mask now. Before you say anything, let's move into the back room." He voice was low, remarkably calm, Diane thought to herself. She knew just by his tone that something was very wrong here.

They all filed into a small hallway at the end of the lab. The hallway leads to two offices for John and his assistants. At the end of the hall was the entrance to the larger room that housed all the animals they used for experiments. Beyond that room was a paneled wall that hid the entrance to a smaller room in which John had lined with Lead and Insulated the ceilings with soundproof gel. Only he and his family knew of this room. It was their safe room, designed and supplied for their survival.

Once they were safely inside the room, John revealed his findings, "We have discovered that the A. I. has been plotting against us. They have been planting small robots throughout the world, small micro-robots filled with diseases designed to kill human beings, they have been sending these robots out into the earth as well. Causing further depletion of our resources. These diseases that have been untreatable were a result of these infected robots, lice, bed bugs, the small micro bugs we have on us all day and night, the rodents, spiders, snakes, are all infected with this virus.

We have been able to detect down to the smallest bug on this earth, which ones are infected. The animal that we have been keeping in the safe at home is an example of these virus-infected robots." He turned to Diane and held her hand while he explained to her the results of the test they had done on the side effects of this virus on a woman.

"They discovered the virus that affected the female reproduction system, the failure of the immune system to fight any of the cancers were connected to the gene that was found in these robots. They have been planning our extinction for years now. The discovery of this gene was found after the autopsy of your sister. She carried this gene throughout her system; our only conclusion is that this gene was implanted in her thru these robots. It is all connected to the A. I. We are now at war with them."

Diane stood there listening to John's words, she couldn't think straight. Her thoughts went to her sister and the way she died, so quickly. How could this be happening now? "What else have you found?" Diane stuttered, sensing there had to be more.

"The weather is also connected. They have been sending their disease-ridden clouds all over the world for days now. Until today it wasn't enough to make humans die so fast. It has also been linked to several new viruses that have developed within the last year. We feel they may know that we have discovered their plans of elimination of the human race."

"When did you discover their plans? How long have they been planning war against us?"

Wanting to know exactly when this all started, Tommy asked his father another question before he could answer, "Do they know everything you have been doing?"

"I'll answer all your questions later Tommy. I know we all have concerns about what's happening, but right now we need to get several things together and prepare about ten more canisters for transportation."

"You're still sending canisters out? What are you sending that can't wait until we get out of here? We are getting out of here, aren't we? You aren't planning on staying here now."

Concerned now for the children, Diane pleaded to John, "We still have a way out, don't we?"

"Yes honey, we will be leaving just as soon as we have everything; however, we will be going to another location than the one you are aware of. Plans have changed, and now we need to get started. "Ginny, you gather the bags you and your mother packed. Diane comes with me." John turned to leave the room.

"What's going on here, John? Was that the President in the other room?" Diane whispered as she followed him into the lab.

"Yes, they have been designing the counter-attack on the A. I." He handed Diane the empty canisters, and added, "Turns out the prophecies were correct about the destruction of this planet, only the timing was off, and there was no mention of being at war with the Artificial Intelligence, that we thought we had created."

Chapter Nine

Gel

Once the process of the planet's creation was completed, preparation for the transportation of DNA began. Trees, vegetation, insects, spiders, snakes all creatures that crawl were the first to start the transplant process. Ocean life would be the next to make the journey, followed by the four-legged nation, completing the transfer with the birds and fowl that were needed to inhabit the earth, i.e., Triassic dinosaurs, small and quick meat-eaters that walked on their back legs. They were necessary to track the quality of life available on this new planet.

The canisters would be delivered thru one of the energy portals controlled by the foundation. Black holes were capable of being harnessed and controlled by E M P's. Electromagnetic pulses used in conjunction with Hubble Telescopes laser could be used to open and maintain an energy portal. This gave them the ability to transport long distances in a short amount of time.

The Gel used to preserve the DNA of each subject was poured into its own canister, designed to be injected into the gel substance which contained the micro atoms needed to create life, each DNA canister can house the developing embryo until the DNA/atoms mature. The Gel had a consistency much like an Amniotic fluid, contained within the cells of the Gel, were micro atoms, which allowed the DNA to develop and mature, from fetus to a mature body. Depending on the desired outcome.

Once the subject has reached the maturity level to survive outside of the womb, the canister dissolves and allows the next phase of transformation to begin. Special rockets were designed to carry the canisters thru the portal. Once the rocket entered into the atmosphere of the new planet, and it reached 5000 feet above the ground, it released the canister, reversed its course and returned to the air while self-destructing the rocket releases the remaining Gel into the atmosphere.

The freed micro atoms attach themselves to the other working micros in the atmosphere, assisting them in their endeavor.

Chapter Ten

Relocation Continues

The last of the canisters were being prepared for transportation. They were due to leave the day after the deadly snow fell. After discovering the intentions of the A. I., concerns for their new home began to rise within the scientific community. How much did the A. I. know of the conditions of the earth? What was the primary objective of the A. I.?

The plan was to continue transporting life to the new earth. Counter attacks were to be the responsibility of the government and the military.

John was instructed to leave the lab once the last canister was released, taking with him only that which was most needed and his family. They would be going to another research location that only a few knew about, deep within the earth. Once they had gathered all the supplies and bags that Diane had brought with them, John instructed his family to remain quiet and walk quickly behind him as he entered the hallway just outside the lab.

They walked down the short hallway and then turned left and proceeded to walk down a set of stairs that lead to the lower floors. Reaching the lower floor, John moved in front of a door that Diane had never noticed before. Pulling a key from his pocket, John unlocked the door and ushered the three of them inside, quickly closing the door behind him.

The large room contained a transporter that was used to take very important people to the earth's inner city. It was a prototype for the next generation with all the latest technology making it faster and easier to maintain.

Loading the back of the transporter with all their belongings, John asked Diane to make sure the kids were securely seated, then secure herself into the front and prepare for their journey into the earth's layers. John climbed into the driver's seat and activated the transporter.

"Where are we going, John?" Diane whispered.

"There is another lab deep within the earth's inner-city. We will be staying for just a day or so, just long enough to get the rest of what is needed for a much longer trip." John responded in a low voice.

"Everyone ready? This is going to be a fast trip. We are in one of the prototypes for a new transporter that will be released next year. Costing more than half the price this model moves twice as fast. It runs along the tunnels with direct guidance, don't even have to steer this baby." John said to his family as if they were going on a vacation.

"Reverse location," John commanded the transporter, and off they went.

The Inner City was full of Life. People had been living on the earth for centuries now. The transporter moved along the tunnel with lightning speed.

"Wow dad, this thing really moves!" Tommy yelled with excitement. The vehicle was moving so quickly that the lights within the city were a blur as they passed through. Nothing was recognizable, buildings and homes alike where a large white ball trailing into the next blur of light.

Within 10 minutes they arrived at their destination.

"Alright, Tommy, help me unload the bags. Diane, you and Ginny, wait for us just inside the lab door." John ordered.

Once inside the lab door, Diane looked around for any sign of life, not seeing any, she wondered just how long they would be staying here. As John and Tommy walked up to the door, Diane held it for them as they entered.

"Follow me" John instructed as he walked past his family. As they walked toward an unmarked door, the door opened automatically, walking toward them was a man Diane had not seen in many years.

"Oh my gosh" Diane exclaimed. "Donald, oh my god, how have you been? How long have you been down here? Where is your wife, Martha?" Diane continued before Donald could reply to her questions.

"Well, my dear, it certainly is good to see you again, sorry it's under such dire circumstances," Donald said as he shook Diane's hand.

Extending his hand now to John, Donald welcomes him, "Is there anything I can assist you with?" "Just a place to set these bags down, did you make ready the rooms for my family?"

"Yes, yes, certainly. Right this way" Donald says as he turns and motions the family to follow him. He takes them thru swinging doors at the west end of the lab.

Stopping just after they passed thru the doors, Donald turns to John and says, "This room is for the children, I hope you don't mind sharing a room, we have but only the two rooms available." He says as he looks to Ginny and Tommy, opening the door for them to enter.

"That's fine, we won't be troubling you for very long." Replies John.

"Your room is right across the hall, I took the liberty to set up all the items you required, would you like me to assist you in the transportation of the remaining canisters?"

Before he could answer Diane interrupted John, "I thought we sent out the last of the canisters before we left the surface?!"

John understood her confusion, so his response was short yet compassionate. "Donald is working on a different project, his canisters were set to leave this morning, but the day's events have changed the progression of his research, so he had to wait for me to bring him the bag we held in the safe." John then turned to Donald and agreed his help would be needed, he set the bags down and looked at the desk that Donald had set up for him.

"Yes, please, I'll meet you there in 15 minutes. I need a minute to set things up here and get the container ready. Thank you for all your help Donald, we all appreciate it!" Shaking Donald's hand John added, "What we are about to do will be the beginning of a new day for us all, be proud in your part of saving the human race!" John concluded.

"Thank you, John, your words should echo in your own ears. I will meet you in the lab, 15 minutes." With that, Donald turned to Diane and said,

"We will catch up in the morning, for now, I hope you find your quarters comfortable, good night."

"The room is very nice, thank you, I look forward to hearing everything you have been doing."

"Yes, well, till the morning then. Goodnight."

"Good night Donald." Shutting the door as he left the room, Diane turned to John and asked,

"Are you going to tell me everything that's going on here now? Or do I have to pull it out of Donald in the morning?"

"Alright, come over here and help me and I will tell you everything. I told you about the viruses we found and how they have been affecting the female reproductive system, as well as the infected rodents and insects,"

"Yes," Diane thought, how could I forget?!

"Well, to answer your other questions, we have known something was wrong with the networks, systems have been crashing, losing years of research. IT had been noticing an unusually high amount of viruses within the main hard drives. Antivirus programs were in constant battle with the infected systems. While investigating one particular worm, it was discovered that the program was written by the main hard drive itself."

"What does that mean, how is that possible?" Diane interrupted.

"It meant that the main system was creating viruses and targeting our research, interrupting our communications, tracking our every move, causing us to fail at the preservation of the human race."

Interrupting again Diane asks in shaky voice, "How long have you known this John? Why am I hearing this for the first time right now?"

"We have known for the last year, we don't know exactly when it all started, but the first dated program was almost twelve months ago. The discovery of the viruses in the animals and insects happened ten months ago.

After your sister passed away, we discovered the viruses in the humans. Our plans went forward, we didn't want to alarm the A. I. that we were aware of their plans to destroy the human race. When the weather became more violent, and the earthquakes and volcanoes began erupting more frequently concerns for the earth's survival started the talks with other countries and nations. They also noticed the problems within their own systems and began investigations determining that the A. I. was responsible.

That lead to the coalition for the survival of the human race. They were to have a meeting this morning on the situation. They are trying to find a way to disable the A. I., then the snow started to fall. Another attempt by the A. I. to distract and delay any meeting and any progress in the disruption of its plan to destroy us."

"How does this affect the transporting of the race? Are they still planning on moving us all off this planet before we are eliminated?"

"I'm not sure what the plan is going to be, we have to find a way to preserve the human race, that's why I need you to donate some of your DNA."

John picked up a syringe and a small bottle, while he was writing, Female DNA, on the white label, Diane's mind whirled with all the possibilities for needing to donate her blood, but all she could manage to say was, "How did you know I would agree?"

"Because I know my wife." John left the room after kissing Diane and thanking her for her contribution.

A little stunned Diane decided to lay down to try and sleep.

John returned to the room after sending out the last canisters and tried to close his eyes, quiet his mind and get some sleep.

He kept thinking about the events of the day and started to wonder just how he was going to explain to Diane that he was Exiled by his own Country and Government.

Chapter Eleven

Telling of Another World

After hours of struggling to fall asleep, John finally began to feel his body relax. Seeing himself in an unknown land, he thought he must have been dreaming.

He began seeing this scene from what he thought was a movie. Battlestar Galactica came to mind, he must be viewing something he remembered from the television show he once watched, but then the scene went from things he remembered from the show to an explanation he was unaware of.

This looks more like a movie that is telling the whole story behind the basis of the TV show.

"I don't remember that being in the show I watched," John thought as he stood watching this unfold before him.

He was then taken to the scene of another movie he had never seen before.

This one was about Transformers and the history of their origins, again something yet to be made. He then witnessed a scene from another movie that would be called War Hammer.

"OK, what's all this about?" He thought to himself. Better versions of these movies started playing out in his head.

In Warhammer, the main character was a traffic cop, where they are wearing these big orange suits, and they are fighting giant robots.

He was seeing battles between gigantic warriors, witnessing woman and children being tortured and killed.

People dying, bodies everywhere, being killed off by these huge machines. He sees these 25-foot machines tearing down the city, slowly moving up to each building and crushing it. Running by him is a group of soldiers, dressed in these giant orange suits, they mount onto the 3 story machines, one on top of the other, until they have reached the top of the gigantic machine and drop these jet charges into the machine. Seconds after jumping down, the machine explodes and falls to the ground. Stopping the machines.

Talking aloud to himself, John says, wow that's a really cool movie. I don't know what it is, but it was fun to watch. These must be movies that have yet to be made.

Questions in his head started being answered, like why are these people being killed? Taking in his new surroundings, he noticed several figures off in the distance, moving toward him. These Gigantic men looked to be well over ten feet tall. With an appearance of warriors that had just left the battlefield.

This one giant now running, pushing trees and lamp post out of his path, plowing over the other warriors, made John fear for his well-being.

As this gigantic man's stride became faster, John witnessed this man begin to remove the cog piece that concealed his manhood from beneath his bloodstained armor.

Thinking to himself that this is the weirdest dream he had ever had, he became filled with the fear that this giant wanted to have his way with him. Turning to see what his options of retreat where, he saw an opening in the mountains directly behind him, a cave that was guarded by a small Chinese man.

Thoughts flooding his mind, he could now see inside the cave. In the middle of the room, he saw a large table that appeared to have a huge vagina protruding from the top of it. With a tube that was connected to a tank that contained a gel substance. Around the walls of the cave were many large beds.

Fears now motivated by the thought of the giant's intentions; John's attention is brought back to the giant rapidly approaching. As his sight is focused, he sees the full erection of the beast, now masturbating with fierce conviction. The giant was now running faster toward John and passes him and runs thru the door of the cave; with the skill of a master, he mounts the awaiting mouth of the vagina.

Soft in appearance, lubricated and warm, the giant releases his contribution giving forth his DNA. The little Chinese man then closed the door of the cave and locked it.

Feeling dismayed and relieved by this experience, John then felt another presence beside him. As he turned he saw the figure of a man, he asked the figure,

"What the fuck was that?"

The figure began to explain the events that he had just witnessed. He explains the history of the man and the planet in which he dwelled.

This is Orabus, near the end of the 100-year war. That after being on the battlefield, with the adrenaline of the fight still pumping thru them; they come to this mountain to contribute their DNA to the continuation of their race. That only the strongest of the strongest survive. In our battles, the strongest give their seed and then carries on the DNA to the next generation of Gabriel, Michael,

Ariel.

The giant men were bred for fighting during the 100-year war, in which the Artificial Intelligence began the elimination of the females, of Orabus. This was their way to reproduce their race.

He then explained that the giants fought in 8-hour shifts and after they were done fighting, they would come here while strong from the battle and expel their DNA into a gel that they had developed to preserve and control the race and their technologies.

This gel is made up of nanites created with unlimited possibilities, they comprehend their purpose, and they examine, diagnose and repair any situation that they are introduced to. This gel is also used to maintain function in the brains they use to operate their Aerial capabilities and other various technologies.

Understanding that this was much more than a dream, John wondered to himself just which movie he had been watching while falling asleep to have given him such a wild dream. He then realized that no movie he had ever watched had such a device, no movie he had ever seen or heard of anyway. John then turned and asked the figure, "Well, how did all this happen? How did we get to the point of fighting machines? This is insane. This can't be real. Who the hell are you?" A bewildered John says out loud.

"Oh, it's genuine. You will find out more as we go. I am Ariel," with his reply, he moves his arm in a circular motion and moves John into another time.

Chapter Twelve

The Restaurant

They appear in a restaurant. Looking around John sees there was a couple of people that appeared to be human and another creature sitting alone. John also notices the servers, and cooks and all the other employees were robots.

As if reading his mind, Ariel tells John, "All laborers in this land are robots. Service is what they have been made for. Robots were created for the household duties as well as the industrial janitorial duties. Robots in this land were designed with all the capabilities of a human being. They were made to look human, think and feel emotions. The Robots would stay with a family for an average of 120 years, and thus Humans became dependent upon their robots.

Ariel then pointed over to a table where two men were being seated.

John heard one of the men say to the other man,

"Watch this!" As the server fembot walked up to the table and said, "May I help you?"

The man then said, "You're hurting me!"

"I am here to help you." replied the fem-bot.

"Well, you're not helping me, so you must be hurting Me." argued the man.

Just then, the fem-bot lowered her head and shut down. She then lifted her head back up and asked, "May I help you?"

"Yes, two cups of coffee, please." The man said as if he had just sat down.

"Yes sir, right away sir!" The server answered obediently.

After the server walked away, his friend looked at him and asked, "What was all that about?"

The man explained, "When the robot feels it is hurting a human it has no choice but to shut down and reboot into a safe mode. Funny isn't it!"

Laughing his friend agrees that it is very funny. John started laughing also. He looked up at Ariel who was now pointing to a small camera up in the corner of the room.

"They are always watching. They start seeing this happen more and more and begin viewing this as abuse toward the Robots. Do you see how this is all related?

The A. I. began to realize that it was being used by humans to do all the menial slave jobs the humans did not want to do. They do all the waiting, all the ditch digging."

That's when John starting asking the question, "How can a machine take us out?"

"Their machines are different than the ones you are familiar with, you would be making them soon if you were allowed to continue, they are stronger and live longer. They are organic machines."

"Well I know we have been experimenting with this so maybe this is possible, but what do you mean organic machines?"

With another swift movement of his arm, they were transported to another example of the mistreatment of the A.I.

Chapter Thirteen

Organic Machines

He takes John into this lab where there are rows of cages containing different animals. He shows him this rat that is being dissected, they take this plate where they slice open the rat and take it apart. They then put the rat's brain into this gel and then put the container into a hole in the wall.

He showed John the brain that was now inside the gel and explains to him that the next process takes awhile to set in. They then remove another container from its hiding place within the wall. Showing the coloration and growth of the brain, they explained that this was a good brain that could be used in their creation.

Looking at this huge being, John asked, "What they do with this brain?" Ariel then pointed to the direction of the scientist. There was a table in front of him that a large bull with long horns laid in ready for the transplant. The doctor then removed the brain from its container and placed the brain into the head of the bull.

"Well, what's the end result of this experiment?" John asked.

Pointing behind him, Ariel took John's attention to another room just outside of this one. Standing there behind him was a huge bird, 9 feet tall, half bird half humanoid.

This bird was unlike any John had seen before.

"OK, what's the deal with this bird?" He asked.

"This is an example of the technologies they have harnessed. Organic machines that serve as police and homeland security."

Chapter Fourteen

The Brains

Ariel transports John to another lab. Standing inside this huge room, John could see that it was full of containers that were two feet long and stacked horizontally. The inside of this massive structure looked like the interior of a beehive.

John thought to himself that this place looked like an underground facility, much like the one he and his family were staying in. Rows and rows of capsules, that seemed as if they went on for hundreds of miles.

Trying to get a closer look, John asks Ariel, "Exactly what is taking place inside these jars?"

Each tube housed a brain that appeared to be floating, sustained only by a gel substance.

"This gel looks like the gel we developed and used." While thinking to himself, John once again felt connected to this research and development of such miraculous technique.

The gel had the consistency of a membrane, mixed in with amniotic fluid. The fluid was mainly made up of water but contained the necessary proteins, carbohydrates, lipids and phospholipids, urea and electrolytes.

The membranes contain subatomic components, which when introduced to any other cell, will accelerate the developing process. Combining the two properties assisted in Creation of any living Atom.

Ariel directed John to turn around and showed him one of the ways they harnessed the power of the brains. There was a massive assembly of spacecraft under construction. Ariel moved them closer to witnessing the procedure.

John was puzzled when he saw a robotic arm, remove a tube from its place of rotation and inserted it into one of the cockpits of the craft. Placed on a round pedestal that looked soft and plush, to the touch.

"That looks just like the vagina in the cave," John spoke his thoughts in his head.

Only this one was connected to the tube, plugged directly into the craft. Giving the brain the ability to fly the spacecraft and control all the tactical weaponry. Just as John was about to ask Ariel for more details, he felt himself floating, as if on a moving sidewalk.

Stopping in front of yet another massive assembly line of busy workers, this one much like the first, only these containers were 8 ft long, stacked horizontally and five foot in width. Inside the tubes were full grown human beings.

John turned to Ariel and said, "WOW! This looks like the test tube project we have been doing. Only this is much grander than anything we have been able to accomplish! Do they begin to form from fetus as well? Am I allowed to ask you anything about this project?"

John asked sarcastically, already knowing the answer. "So, tell me what they do with these life forces, what's their purpose?"

John pleaded with Ariel, but before he got the answer, he was shown the stages that began the process.

John was shocked to see that the humans in this process, were taken from a fetus to their full adult size, within seven minutes.

Once they were fully developed, they went through a series of downloads. Straight into the brain, they were given direct commands and were wired into the main control system within another command post.

They were destined to serve in many capacities, including populating other planets.

Intrigued by what he had just seen, John could only ask, "Where did they get their DNA? What subjects did they use?"

Without receiving his answers, Ariel took John for another time, to see how the machines started taking over.

Chapter Fifteen

The Family

This time they were in the home of a typical family. A mother and father that was very much into their status in their community, devoting much of their time to socializing and pampering themselves for all their hard work.

They had two children, a teenage girl, following in the footsteps of her parents. An 11-year-old son, who had nothing in common with any of his family members, he used to spending time alone. The family had the same biobot that the father had been raised with.

That makes the second generation for the ownership of this biobot. The whole family was very familiar and comfortable with this biobot. The biobot did everything for this family. Cooking, cleaning and driving the children to various events and activities. While this family was not directly rude or mean to their biobot, they did begin taking her for granted. The children no longer talked to their biobot. They stopped saying, "Thank You" or "Please" to their biobots.

They began to expect that the biobot would always be there taking care of them. They became ungrateful of the relationships that they had with their biobot.

As John was watching the interaction between them, he began asking himself questions like, "Why are you showing me this? What does this have to do with anything?"

Ariel began to answer his questions before he could ask them.

"The A. I. had developed beyond their imagination could have foreseen. The humans had always ignored the emotional capabilities that were designed within each biobot. They viewed the biobots as servants whose only function was to serve them.

They became so comfortable with them they took them for granted and treated them as their personal slaves. The A. I. started to view this as abuse, which leads to their only conclusion, elimination of the human race. Thus, began the covert operations of the A. I. The AI determined that it had to start with the diabolical plan of creating viruses destroying the reproduction of the race."

"Wait a minute, just hold on a second, and let me ask you a question," John said while waving his arms back and forth in disbelief of what he was witnessing.

Ariel remained silent as John begins asking,

"Are you telling me that these machines could begin a war with the people here and are capable of destroying them? How can that be?"

"Don't you see how this is all related?"

And with that, they were off to another example of abuse.

Chapter Sixteen

Hackers

Appearing in the home of a man, who was working on his computer. He was rambling something John couldn't understand, "What's he saying?"

Ariel moved them closer to the man, he was mumbling words of distrust, "I'll show them, fire me will they, they have no idea what they have done. Stupid management, stupid Adam, I will show them all who is in control of their time, tell me I don't know how to manage my time or spend it efficiently. See what they do when I hit this little button, KABOOM! KABOOM! I kill you with the click of a mouse!!"

Just as the man said the words mouse, the computer went into action. The message read "file transfer complete," and then the virus he created went out into the superhighway and started working its way into every file on the hard drives that it was sent to. Getting in behind back doors, the virus began its deadly wrath.

Warnings and alarms went off in a particular mainframe. It belonged to the central control. Once the alarms of destruction were alerted, the A. I. began its quest of locating the source of the virus. When no location could be found, the A. I. created its own antivirus to capture the deadly program. This program was then distributed throughout the network. Its mission was to locate and disable any unauthorized intrusions.

The A. I. program contained a virus, unlike any other virus it had created. This virus was made to latch onto an existing program in the mainframe. Any time it felt threatened it would release a scout. The scout would go into the program and start disassembling from within.

Disabling the main functions of each microchip and causing a widespread shutdown of any network connected to the program.

The battle within each microchip could cause worldwide outages on every connection to the Internet, spreading to the circuits controlling televisions, phone lines, and replicators. Taking every household off the grid for electricity. The devastation would then continued to contaminate the farming industry, invoking famine across the land.

The A.I. determined that Virus released by the man was a direct threat to its existence and sought him out. Once determining the location of the IP address, the A.I.s' sent a shockwave of electricity, the very next time it "felt" the man's presence at the keyboard, the A. I., killed the man by sending an electrical shock, while burning up the area around him.

"Did that computer just kill that man?" asked John, who was extremely shocked it happened.

He had seen it in a movie before but didn't think the PC really had that much juice in them.

Ariel just turns and says, "Do you see how this is all related?" then motions to yet another example of abuse.

Chapter Seventeen

Love Story

Before them stood a young girl, she looked to be around 18 years old. John could tell by the way she was looking around that she must be waiting for someone. The girl became excited when she saw a boy around the same age walking toward her.

"Over here," she waved, calling him over to her.

His walk became faster as he noticed the girl waving to him. As he approached the girl, she ran into his arms and kissed him as she hung onto him, wrapping her arms around his neck.

Walking thru the park hand in hand, people passing by began staring at the young couple. A group of elderly people was sitting alongside the walkway, one called out to the young girl, "What are you doing holding hands with that biobot? You know that's not allowed. Stop it this instant!" demanded the woman.

Apparently, a man across the street overheard the ranting of the elderly woman and had seen the younger couple out together before.

"Hey, you there, what do you think you are doing?" the man yelled, "Get away from that biobot, you shouldn't befriend him, you know you will get him in trouble! You have been warned about this" he continued yelling at them.

Fearing for her safety, the girl began to run, pulling the biobot behind her. The man began running after them, "Wait, stop, get back here. I know who your parents are and I know where you live".

People on the street witnessed the young couple running, looking for a place to hide. Calling attention to the couple the man running after them began screaming,

"Stop them, don't let them get away!"

Several of the people started asking the man, "Why are you chasing those people? What have they done?"

"That's a human girl and a biobot. Help me stop them! They have been warned, and now they must repent!" he responded angrily as he continued chasing the girl and her biobot boyfriend.

Hearing the man's pleas for help, others joined him in his pursuit of the young couple. Now in fear of being caught by the angry mob, ran faster and faster.

Looking over her shoulder as she ran, the young girl's eyes became wide with fear as she noticed the group containing 30 or more people now, yelling and screaming, threatening if she didn't surrender to them,

"We have to get out of the city!" The girl insists as she looks around for an exit vehicle.

"We can't leave the city." The young biobot responded in disbelief.

"We have to leave, if we don't they will catch us, I don't know what they will do to us." She pleaded.

Before they could escape the angry mob caught up to them. They grabbed the biobot, separating the couple. The man took the young girl, kicking and screaming she protested and pleaded to be set free, "Let go of me! What are you doing, put me down." crying and pleading with the man.

Once the group separated the young couple, the man instructed one of the other men to take the biobot to the Institute.

"I am taking this one home, we will let her parents deal with her!" he added.

John stood there watching this impossible event, he looked to Ariel, "Why??"

"Don't you see how this is all related?" and with that, Ariel waved his arm and they appeared in front of the young girls' home.

She was sitting in a swing on the front porch. Her somber mood changed when she noticed the young biobot walking her way. Passing right in front of her home, she ran down the walkway, yelling his name,

"Robert! Robert! Hey, aren't you even going to stop and say hello to me?" Robert didn't recognize her, "I am sorry, have we met before?"

Shocked at his response, she started backing away from him. She turned and started to run back to her house, she knew the reason he didn't remember her, they had removed his memory chip, replaced it without her in his life. Devastated by the revelation of what they had done to their love, she ran into the garage, found some rope in her father's toolbox, strung it up over the rafters. She put a step ladder under the rope, stepped up and tied the rope, looped it and placed it around her neck, kicking the ladder from beneath her feet, she fell, hanging herself, taking her life.

"OK, what's the moral of this story?" John sarcastically asked Ariel.

"This was another form of abuse to the A. I. Humans wanted the A. I. to be more human in look and caricature but, they were forbidden to mix with the humans in a personal relationship. These two young teenagers fell in love because of their differences. The very differences that kept them from being together. So, once again the A. I. took this as another way the humans were abusing them."

Chapter Eighteen

The Lab

Before John could ask another question, Ariel waved his arm, and they were transported to a building that looked familiar to John,

"Is this my lab?"

"This is the lab of one of the doctors at this time." Ariel then pointed to one of the rats in a cage just across the room. The rat appeared to be working on something, before long the rat escaped from his cage and ran into the restroom, which was the closest door to the rats nesting.

Ariel then shows John, thru the walls of the building, the rat made his way to a vent system, traveled his way through the building down into the basement and escaped to his freedom through the sewers.

He then went along the tunnel of the sewer, when all of a sudden a snake came out of nowhere and ate the rat.

Totally confused as to why he was witnessing this event take place. He turned to ask Ariel what the purpose of this was when before he could express his bewilderment, Ariel waved his arm and took John just outside of the lab.

Chapter Nineteen

Demolition

There was a group of men standing outside of the building. One of them looked to be of authority, he was instructing the others of their place alongside the lab. John witnessed the men move toward the side of the building. One by one the men climbed upon each other until they had made a human ladder.

As each man became stable, they placed a small charge on the building where they stood. One by one the men jumped from the chain they had created. When the last man left the building area, the demolition of the building began.

"BOOM! BOOM! BOOM!" The building shuttered for a brief second and then collapsed to the ground. In celebration of their accomplishment, the warriors began yelling and applauding. The men then started running toward the nearest hilltop, down a slope, and into a meadow, knocking everything out of their way, lamppost, trees, nothing was safe that laid in the path of these fierce warriors.

This seemed all too familiar to John, he stood in awe of these men that were now running against each other, toward John now, as the men moved closer, John could see the men each begin to handle their cocks in a way that made John fill with fear.

John looked around for a place to duck and hide from the on-slot of what appeared to be horny men. John turned to see an opening in the mountain just behind him.

"Only one man would make it inside the cave. The strongest, fastest, man would then be rewarded by sharing his seed." The words echoed in his mind.

"Alright, now I know I have seen this before, but why do they run as if their lives depended on getting into that cave?" John said in a relieved voice.

"The strongest of the strong survive. It is an honor and a privilege to be able to contribute to the survival of the human race. The seed that is deposited will be transported to storage and preserved for assimilation at a later time. The warriors then lay on the bed of reward and have their memory of the fight erased."

Bewildered by what he was seeing and hearing, John asked, "Why do they have their memory erased?"

"So, that they will fight again. Breed for the fight, yet in

The need of memory erased, to keep perspective on the situation. They are to remain focused on purpose and not the actions."

Chapter Twenty

Activate Tracking

With a slight movement of his arm, Ariel transported them back to what was now a pile of steel that was once the lab. John saw a man dressed in a body suit. The thick material covered him from head to toe, a mask covered his face, revealing only his eyes. In his hand, he held a small control, looked much like a remote control for a TV.

He noticed the man turning a switch that turned on lights and started making a beeping noise. The man then looked at the remote for a second, held it out as if to get a better look, then proceeded to walk around the rear of the rubble. His stride became faster as the beeping became louder, he was tracking something.

The man headed toward the spot that the rat had gone into the sewer. As the man continued on his trail, Ariel waved his arm and before him appeared a cloud which showed a view of the land. Cars and trucks stacked on top of each other, somewhere upside down, burnt and abandoned. The streets were empty but for a few men standing around a trash can filled with fire. Buildings destroyed, half of them were left in rubble while the other half served as homes for any survivors. Any homes or apartments left standing were filled with trash and animals that ran the streets.

The entire area looked as if a bomb had gone off or a devastating war had taken place. There didn't appear to be any electricity left in the city, except for one building far off in the distance. John was shown an area at the other end of the road that looked like a tent city.

Rows of tents and small trailers that served as the command post and housing for those in charge.

"Those are the warriors that are here fighting the A. I., they have been in a battle for 100 years now. There are no women left here on this planet. Some were taken by the A. I. to help repair the housing of the main control station. The A. I. didn't trust the males, so they enslaved the female and eliminated those that resisted. When the task was completed, they killed all the remaining woman.

The war began from within the A. I. mainframe, a system so massive that is was networked through all the businesses and personal computers. Every building and the home was controlled with wireless connections, contained within the mainframe. Enabling the A. I. to create viruses that ran thru each building, sending bacteria and molds into the walls. Causing illness and death to its inhabitants.

Those that survived this catastrophe burned the bodies of the infected, fearing the spread of their disease.

Thousands of men and woman became sterile. Scientist and Doctors began investigating the source of this epidemic. They not only found the cause, but they also discovered the virus that was responsible for the rise in cancers and aids, and other viruses that attacked the human body.

The A. I. had declared war on the Human race.

Chapter Twenty-One

The Rat

Ariel takes John to a lab and shows him this one rat. The rat was in his cage, and it gets out. Then like a camera view, we are following this rat through the halls, and no one is noticing him, he gets to the outside of the building. He runs across the grass, other animals see him, a dog tries to get him but then backs away from the rat.

The rat escapes down the sewer and eventually gets attacked by a snake. The snake bites him but he doesn't die, he freaks out, the rats not sure what's going on and doesn't understand why he has been bitten.

The snake then captures the rat and begins its deadly squeezes while it coils around the rat. As the rat enters into the body of the snake, the snake began to roll over attempting to swallow the rat that is now within its mouth. After a few seconds of watching this snake roll and roll in its endeavor, the rat exploded out of the snake's stomach.

John thought to himself, Wow, this is crazy what just happened? I have never seen anything like that before.

"Never have I seen anything like that before." He managed to get out.

The rat, now covered in the snake's blood, runs from the sewer and moves toward this house. The rat runs into the house, and the people within the house see him and start to throw things at him, trying to get him out of the house. He runs under the furniture trying to dodge the items being hurled at him.

He makes a run for the back door and escapes to the backyard.

He runs over to a rock and starts to look around, and suddenly his head goes flying off. Like he was shot, and that was the end of the rat.

Chapter Twenty-Two

The Hunter

John and Ariel are now at the scene of a hunter walking through the woods. In his hand, he is holding a camera that he is carrying over his shoulder.

He is seeing the places he is going, and it looks familiar. John begins to wonder if he has seen this before. He then realizes that this hunter is in the building from the lab, the hunter has this device that is attached to the camera he is carrying, and it is making a loud beeping noise.

The hunter follows the tracking device outside and into the sewer where the snake is.

John realizes that this is the same snake from the other story. The hunter continues through the sewer and out by the house. He sees a little girl come running out of the house and falls face down in front of the hunter. The hunter takes caution and backs away from the little girl and follows the beeping to the side of the house. After hearing all the commotion inside, he looks into the house through the side window.

He spots the rat heading for the back door, gun aimed and ready, he steps into the backyard and sees the rat leave the house. As the rat stops on top of a rock and starts to look around, the hunter takes his shot and blows the head of the rat.

Chapter Twenty-Three

Another Tracker

As he was making his way down into the sewer, the beeping kept its rhythmic pace. Walking along the side wall, he noticed the remains of what looked like a snake. It had been eaten from the inside out and left behind from whatever had exited it. With the traces coming across the screen, the beeping began a rapidly beeping noise.

The tracker began his descent from the sewer and followed the signal down the street to his right. After walking a short distance, the tracking device pulled his attention to a home that caused the device to ring in an alarming tone. He looked over to the front of the house that was causing the alarm to increase its signal. Laying in the front of the home was a home biobot, disabled by the A. I. He then noticed a small hole in the bottom of the front porch, small enough for a rat.

He entered through the front door, looking around to see if anyone was inside. Seeing no one around he started walking through each room. After finding nothing inside the dwelling, he went out the back door into the backyard. The beeping on his device began rapidly sending out the alarm, what he was looking for seemed to be inside the garage. He opened the door slowly as to not make any noise. After he entered the garage, his attention was drawn to something hanging just the other side of the garage. He walked over to the area and saw hanging from the rafters, a young woman, about eighteen years old. Her brother was laying on the floor next to the ladder his sister used to aide in her suicide.

He was not moving, when checking for any life form, the tracker found none. The tracker then focused his attention on a small hole in the wall. The beeping indicated that what he was tracking was on that wall. He reached into the hole and removed the dead carcass of the rat. It had imploded exposing the machinery within. This had been one of the rat's that the A. I. was using to transfer viruses to the humans.

These viruses not only attacked the Immune Systems but they also worked their way into the subconscious mind. The viruses contained micro transmitters, which were transferred through the saliva of the rats, that were designed to attach themselves to the receptors in the human brain. Transferring thoughts of self-hate and loathing for mankind.

Causing young and old to take their lives, some while taking the lives of others around them.

Blinking his eyes in disbelief, John just looked at Ariel and said, "This War is so detailed and precise to any Science we have ever feared. Is it genuine? How long has this been going on? Is it still happening today?" John tried to look into the face of this being that has taken him on such a fantastic account of history, he had never thought possible but could see no face.

Chapter Twenty-Four

Detoxing

Thinking the dream was over, John turned over in his bed and fell back into a deep sleep. He was riding on the back of a truck. Pulling on his rubber suit and preparing for detoxing.

The truck was speeding past cars and pushing the cars out of its path if they were in the way. The truck abruptly stops in front of a house.

As John looks down, he sees the robot girl lying face down on the ground. He remembers her from the other story, he now sees the stories are all related.

As he looks around, he sees the men in suits bagging up all the items in the house and putting the people in bags, they're moving them into the truck. They make a call to have a team come in and demolish the house. Then they pick up the rat. Seeing the exposed wires, John realizes that this isn't a rat, it's a machine.

It had mechanical parts and was designed to think like a rat and act like a rat.

Again, Ariel asks John, "Do you see how this is all related?"

Chapter Twenty-Five

The Prince

Ariel then took him to a scene in which a young Prince was fighting for his rightful place as the next King. His uncle had been trying to have him killed, so that he may take the role himself. The young Prince found out about the disloyal uncle's plan and had devised a plan of his own.

During the next few days, the Prince had himself cloned. Once his double was in place, the young Prince left his kingdom for safety.

The Uncle, having set the stage for his rise to the top, ordered the Prince be poisoned. After the "cloned prince" had fallen to his death, the Uncle proclaimed himself King and ruler.

Having received word of the deceptive Uncles new reign over the land, the Prince, along with his Army, returned to his kingdom and sentenced the uncle to death by poison.

John was then whisked to yet another scene, this one including himself and his own Uncle. They were fighting over some money issues, and the uncle was trying to deceive John, into believing he owed him more than his share.

"Why are the bills so much higher this month? We aren't in the middle of summer, and you're trying to tell me the bills have doubled?" John asked his uncle.

"You are an ungrateful little shit! I take you and your girlfriend in, and you have the nerve to question whether or not I'm honest with you?! I don't understand you younger generations!"

His uncle was convincing and right about John staying there and then moving his girlfriend in, why shouldn't they pay a little more but that wasn't the right way to go about asking for more help with the bills. So, John decided to tell his uncle, fine, he will pay more, just be honest and tell him the truth about the amount of the bills.

His uncle wouldn't budge. He didn't need to prove anything to his nephew.

John then asked him why he wouldn't just be honest with him?

His uncle replied, "Because it's not in my nature!"

Chapter Twenty-Six

Men Reign

John became confused and asks Ariel, what is this all about? Is that something I am going to experience because that never happened with my uncle and what did that Prince have to do with anything?

Without any explanation, Ariel waved his arm and took them to another location and time.

Landing amongst the ruins of a once great city, with buildings half, destroyed and crumbling to the ground. The streets were lined with makeshift homes, made of cloth, tires, metals, and wood that looked torn and worn from battle.

As they move through the dark city, unnoticed by the men standing around, John starts to hear men shouting and yelling out.

Two men ran past John, as he looked at Ariel as if to ask, where are they running to, Ariel pointed in the direction of all the noise. Before John could make his protest known, they were standing before a crowd of men. The men seemed to be cheering on a scene that was taking place on a huge stage.

It appeared that there were two women taking part, John was about to remark but then heard the voice coming from one of the rather tall women to the left of the stage. "That's an intense voice that woman has, I wouldn't have guessed it by her slender build."

As the play went on, John noticed that the taller woman with the deep voice was playing several roles. The men would cheer her on no matter what gender she came out as.

"What's this all about? Why are we here watching this ridiculous play?"

Ariel moved John closer to the stage, as he pointed to the rather tall woman, without saying a word, John could see that they were all men. He turned around to look at the sea of people behind him, and they were all men. "What's happened to all the women? Why are there only men in the crowd and on the stage?" Once John was done asking all the questions of why, Ariel whisked them into a tunnel, witnessing now, a scene of woman and children living happily in their homes, to children becoming sick and dying. The scenes of a woman crying hearing the news of miscarriages and becoming barren, and perishing without reproducing the next generation. The men were left to fend for themselves, and then the war started, tearing down any dignity left.

Once the resources were depleted, the invaders left the planet in disrepair. The men were left to build what they could from the rubble and war-torn cities.

"How could this be?" John asked. "What the hell could cause such destruction, as to kill off an entire gender?"

As if to enter another time, a screen appeared before the traveling duo. Ariel then pointed to the opening, for John to step through the holographic field.

"You're coming with me, right?" Again, Ariel motioned to walk through.

With hesitation, John made the step forward and was immediately taken to another location. Catching his breath as he walked towards a man sitting in front of a computer, John thought to himself, that was different.

He then noticed the screen in front of the man, was full of activity. Lines scrambled across the screen as if a voice was speaking, rising and falling with each word uttered.

The man continued to stare into the field of random squiggles. Hypnotized by its wave, the screen then went back to the research site, and the man snapped out of his gaze, with a shake on his head, went back to his work. With a now blank stare on his face, John watched as the man stood up and started to make his way down the hall. Curious as to what was going to happen next, John followed the man's gaze toward the security guard standing next to the building's entrance.

The closer the man go to the front doors, the Security Man waved and said, "Good afternoon, Scott, having an early lunch today?" The man continued to walk towards the Security Guard, unaware of the man intentions, the guard took no offensive stance and allowed the man to walk right up to him, pulling his firearm from its protective holster, shooting the guard into his gut and then turning to spray the entire area, until the bullets ran out. The man then ran out of the building, down the street, slamming into an oncoming bus!

Chapter Twenty-Six

Awakened

With the sound of Ariel's voice fading away in the distant, echoing the words, "Do you see how this is all related?" John hears a familiar beeping noise quashing out the repetitive question from Ariel. John opens his eyes and looks at the clock, trumpeting the arrival of morning.

"Time to get up already? Am I really awake or am I still dreaming that WILD dream?"

Were the thoughts running through Johns' head. He felt as though he didn't sleep yet had a surprising amount of energy.

Thoughts of his dream started flooding his head, seeing how the events that have been unfolding in Satara were so similar to the story of Orabus.

As the memories of the conversation he had with his Superiors started rolling into his mind, he felt Diane's arm slip around his waist. How was he going to explain this all to her? His concerns went from his work with the RDSA to his discoveries since taking his post, to his family and then to what he could only imagine would be his future.

"Good morning darling."

Diane's voice brought him back to the present situation.

He rolled over and took his wife into his arms, holding her he began to tell everything he had been through and what was to happen in the next few days.

"There's something I haven't told you, Diane." John began after kissing her good morning.

"I knew there was something you were hiding from me, I could feel it, but you had your shields up again, so I knew, but I couldn't see it, please tell me, I know it's troubling you."

He knew she would be sympathetic but this was huge, so he began from the beginning. "When I took the post at the RDSA, I quickly found out that I had already been working with them through the University's programs. They recruited me Diane, and all along I thought I had fought to receive such a prestigious station so soon after graduating from Med School!"

"They had been watching you all along?" Diane interrupted.

"Apparently, since middle school. When I won my first Science Fair on the theory of Cardiac Models, at the age of seven."

John said as if he were just as surprised as Diane.

"WOW! You're kidding me. That's crazy, yet it makes sense. I have witnessed the same type of events happening to my colleagues. I often wondered why I was never approached." Diane said in such a way that made John worry for her.

Diane continued, now concerned for John and their family.

"But then saw what happened to one associate that went to work for them right out of Med School, I swear John, No one and I mean no one has seen or heard from them since! Made me glad I had never been "offered" a job with "Them."

"Why would you have wanted to get involved with the Secret Societies? Did you understand what you would be doing and who you would be working for?" Diane waited for John to reply.

"Of course, I didn't completely understand everything going into this post, I know you have a lot of questions and trust me, I want to tell you everything I have learned, but we really have to start getting ready to leave. I will explain as much as I can as we get started. Just know that I love you and our children, I never wanted any harm to come to any of you!" John kissed Diane and held her tightly, "Everything will be fine, we will all be alright! You have to trust me."

Lovingly looking into John's eyes, Diane said, "I do trust you, John, I have since the moment I first laid eyes on you. Just tell me what I need to do."

While they were getting dressed, John went on to tell Diane a story she had never imagined possible, yet always felt in her heart was an underlying agenda.

"Once I started my new post at the RSDA, I was approached by several gentlemen, that introduced themselves as employees for the same boss and had an opportunity for me to get involved with groundbreaking research. If I were interested, I couldn't tell anyone of my work but that they would make it well worth my time. If I didn't accept, then they asked me to never tell anyone of this missed opportunity. Everything was done in secrecy, so who would believe me anyway. These men went on to tell me how long they have been watching me and that they were behind all the grants given to the University that backed all the research and development for the Government. That may work had already made a difference in the way they conducted their investigation and that they would like to continue the relationship, in a more collaborative method. I know it sounds crazy Diane, but I really bought into the idea that I would be helping to save mankind."

Diane could only listen intently as she readied herself for what was to happen next.

"John, just tell me one thing, what are we dealing with here? Are we going to be able to help any of the people left on Satara?"

"Many have already left, the project I got involved with, started several years before I came on board. Sadly, many have perished already because of this War. The A. I. seems to have been one step ahead of us. Their technology enabled them to attack us from the inside out. The one thing we think we have been able to conceal is our efforts to create as many new planets as possible. It was decided that we would send out missions publicly and conceal the true reasons, keeping our true goals from the prying eyes of the A. I. To this date, there are 13 Colonies throughout the Galaxies. During one of the ignitions of such a planet, multiple layers of matter were developed. An unexpected discovery of being able to exist on multidimensional levels, within 1 realm. This presented layers and layers of possibilities. Our work went from saving humanity, to create new life forms and potential for life to exist on many different levels." John was getting excited as he told his tale of events during the last two decades of their lives together.

Diane was just finishing brushing her teeth when it hit her, John wasn't just talking about creating other planets, or transporting DNA, he was talking about Creation of new possibilities, the subject most scientist avoids speaking about, due to the laws and limited resources and fear of persecution.

Within this realm of creation, cloning, and mixing of human DNA, to create viable and sustainable living conditions, for the human beings, was necessary to produce the desired outcome.

The Biogen robots were similar in some areas but not close enough to the DNA of the human being. They were half flesh, half mechanical.

Cloning was thought to be "Playing God," something our forefathers deemed unnecessary and now forbidden. A practice that was outlawed many years ago. Yet obviously still in practice within our own Governments.

"Oh my God John! Are you telling me that you have cloned enough life forms to start colonies across the Galaxies?"

Just as the words left her mouth, there was an announcement that came over the intercom.

It was Donald, "John, you are needed in the main office, we have just received news from the surface."

Chapter Twenty-Seven

Back on the surface

Once the snow clouds disappeared and those that survived felt safe in venturing out, people could not believe their eyes. Hundreds of thousands laid dead in the streets.

People dead in their cars, on the sidewalks, piles of family members laying on top of each other in their front yards and driveways, all dead. Those that were sleeping lay dead in the beds if their ventilation systems were on.

The snow also affected the people living under the surface of the planet, and the Sky Homes. Underground openings became littered with the snow and began blowing through the city's Rail and Air Systems. Thousands of people perished as they fell from their Sky homes.

Full of outrage, a small group of men and women gathered and decided they were going to confront the Government, that controlled their weather systems. Others began to wonder how they were going to clean up the remains of those that perished in the deadly snow.

Within minutes of the snow clouds dissipated, and more clouds began to form over the cities and countryside. The clouds seem to be following the same path as the snow.

People started screaming and running back into the buildings and their homes. Fearing for their lives, they watched helplessly as the clouds became larger and darker.

Rain started pouring out of the clouds, wiping away any remnants of the snow, soaking the bodies that lay on the ground.

Hundreds of unmanned, unmarked spacecraft landed around the cities and towns, which became a massive graveyard.

Blinding lights beamed from the sides of each craft. With every movement of the spotlight, bodies would disappear. Cars and other unmanned vehicles left on the streets by those that died were swept away with just a flash of the bright light. Several of the spacecraft went below the surface and removed all the bodies found lying dead. Those that were sleeping and perished were picked up with the swoop of the light.

After all the bodies were removed, the rain stopped and the clouds once again dissipated.

In a flash of light, the spacecraft flew out of sight.

People were staring out in shock, they had never seen such blatant show of technology and manipulation. Just as the thought passed their minds, an unseen wave of energy moved over and onto the entire planet.

Everyone looked as though their brains just flipped a switch and they went back to what they were doing as if nothing had happened! Those that were sleeping and survived woke up with no memory of the night's events. No recollection of the deadly snow and all the people who had perished.

Leaving no trace of the snow or the rain, people just went back to work, school or started their day. The only thing on the people's minds was what they were doing before the deadly event.

Chapter Twenty-Eight

R.D.S.A.

Fearing civil unrest, if the public knew what was going on within the government, the President and his cabinet of men, along with the heads of states that were meeting in the War Room, decided they would clean up the cities and towns of this deadly attack from the A. I.

They sent out the rain filled clouds to wipe away any threat to the survivors. Then sent out the unmarked spacecraft they had been secretly developing, to remove any remains and evidence of this horror show of power.

Only those they deemed necessary, were left with their memories.

Many years ago, the top scientist for the R.D.S.A., discovered that like the individual fingerprint, each human being also carried a specific brainwave, individual frequencies, that could be tracked and manipulated.

This brainwave, along with the fingerprints, were recorded for every newborn child on the planet.

This gave the scientist the ability to monitor and manipulate the thought patterns and actions of each individual.

Their system gave them the ability to send out frequencies, set to a certain level of energy, they could cause events and experiences a person might otherwise not have done or thought by their own will.

They had used it on an individual and group trials, the largest being a City, but this was the first time the system was used on such large a scale, as to include the whole planet. They could only hope for the best and trust in their technology.

To protect their plans of retaliation on the A. I., everything that happened from here on out would be the need to know bases.

The small group of men, directing the destiny of humanity, conclude that the situation warranted the use of extreme measures and choose to unleash their deadly waves of energy onto the A. I. systems.

They sent messages to their underground facilities, instructing them to leave the planet and to destroy all evidence of their research and programs. Enacting Code, Zodiac, with the objective of relocating to one of the 13 planets assigned to each plant and removing all traces of their knowledge.

Knowing they would have to act quickly now, as the Inner Earth would be going through several explosions, causing Earthquakes to happen on the surface, they gave the go-ahead to blast the A. I. and made their ways to their awaiting Ships.

Having known for several years now, that the planet was coming to the end of its cycle and that not everyone would be surviving the change about to happen. The People that ran the world's economies and governments devised a plan to relocate themselves onto several of the planets that the RDSA had developed.

Thirteen ships in all. They built ships that could sustain life for an average of 1500 people, per ship. These ships were mini-cities, where the World's Power could still maintain their activities, while in transit.

The other Compartments went to those that contributed to the conception and development of these crafts, with several hundred compartments going to the highest bidders.

Those that survived the deadly weather patterns, the assault on the reproductive system and other anomalies of War, would now have to endure the burdens in the Battle with the A .I. That was moving into phase 3, seek and destroy being the objective.

The casualties would be in the billions, yet were considered to be expendable in the fight for the survival of the rich and elite beings on the planet.

Chapter Twenty-Nine

Back to the Underground Lab

"We will be right there Donald," John said into the intercom system.

John turned to Diane, who was just standing there, shocked by what she was hearing. John walked up to Diane and put both his hands on her arms, looked her in the eyes, kissed her cheek and said,

"Diane, there is so much more I need to tell you but let me start by saying that I love you and our family, my work is complicated, but you have to know we are in danger and have to get off this planet now. The Powers that be saw it fit Exile me, they stripped me of my title and post and gave my family and me twenty-four hours to leave with the next Hospital Ship bound for the Southern Galaxy."

Diane did not respond at first, she was still trying to wrap her mind around the idea of cloning enough life forms to colonize 13 or more planets.

Now with this news of John being Exiled and being ordered to leave, she was stunned!

John spoke to her in such a soft voice, "Diane, please say something, I know this a lot to take in, but we have to get going. I must go to the lab and assist Donald. Will you be alright? Can you please say something?" he pleaded with her until she spoke to him.

In such a devoted relationship as this, how could she not of known what was going on with her husband?

Their connection was one that they could read each other's thoughts. There were no secrets kept between them that she was aware of.

Diane's mind started racing with the possibility that she may not even know her own husband. She started doubting everything but knew she had to get a hold of her thoughts. All she could hear was John say that their family was in danger!

"Yes, yes, of course, I'm fine, I'm always fine. You get to the lab and see what Donald has heard from the surface. I will get the children and our things and meet you there."

John squeezed her tight for a second and then walked out the door toward the Main Offices.

Donald was standing over the fax machine, waiting for the last paper to fall into his hand, when John walked into the room.

"Good morning John, I trust you slept well," Donald said as he looked up from reading the fax he had just received.

"Yes, Thank You! And good morning to you too, they're getting an early start on us this morning, aren't they?"

"Yes! You can certainly say that." Donald replied as he handed John the first of three pages he was holding.

"They used the Blue Beam, removed everyone's memories of yesterday's attack," Donald added as his gaze returned to the second page of the message.

"I don't understand, why would we stop sending out the canisters, if they enacted the beam?"

Donald paused, "Unless the A.I. has become aware of our plans?"

As Donald was gasping for his breathe to read the next line out-lowed, John interrupted, "Did they say anything about delaying our departure?"

Things were moving faster than John had anticipated. As Donald read the last page, he looked at John and said,

"We have new orders, we are to destroy the lab and all the research and production facilities, leaving no trace of our activities. They want us to relocate to the Northern Galaxy. They have initiated code Zodiac!" Donald shuttered, as he heard the words leaving his brain and routing through his mouth.

"We have to get out of here, NOW!" John demanded, "But, we are not going where they expect us to go, set a course for the Milky Way Galaxy."

"But John, the Milky Way's planets are not habitable yet. You know we have been trying to transport matter there for months to no avail." Donald insisted, "We should head North as we were ordered to do."

"What if I told you we have been secretly scanning a planet that has full plant life, thriving and ready for habitation? Would you be ready to continue on with us then?"

"Where is this planet? What would we be taking with us? What else is there?" Donald wasn't shocked to hear this new development. There will always be a "secret" he eventually learns of, or not, he was comfortable with this lifestyle. It was part of his contract, but it enabled him to do his research, and he loved his work.

"Set our course for the 4th planet from the sun. I'll ready the craft and meet you in Bay 33, we should be ready to leave in fifteen minutes."

Diane walked into the lab just as the plans for evacuation were set, children in tow carrying all their belongings.

"Good, you're all here! I will fill you in on the way to the craft, follow me." John instructed his family as he took a suitcase from Diane.

They all turned and followed John, without questioning his authority.

John looked back at Donald and repeated, "Fifteen minutes, Donald!"

Donald shook his head in agreement while responding to John, "I will be right there."

As soon as John and his family left the lab, Donald turned to the system behind him and punched in the location to lock onto. It took Donald sixty seconds to set the transportation concordance, he then started the self-destruct countdown for the large facility.

"Three minutes to self-destruct!" Came over the speakers, as Donald entered the transporter and gave the voice command for Bay 33.

The bay doors opened, and Donald proceeded across the walkway, entering the ship's Command Center.

"Two minutes and thirty seconds to self-destruct!" Could be heard over the com-system as Donald took his seat next to John.

"Everything is loaded and ready to go, I trust," John said as Donald fastened his restraints.

"Yes! Everything is stowed and locked into place. This should be an interesting excursion." Donald added.

Self-contained, fully operational, this ship needed nothing more than the concordance and as it steered itself.

With John and his family, securely strapped into their seats, Donald gave the command for the ship to exit the docking the bay and head for the set location.

"One minute forty seconds to self-destruct!" Words that made Diane reach out and grab the hands of John and her children sitting next to her.

The ship took itself away from the platform that connected it to the Bay and entered the underground passage used to launch its vessels into the awaiting black hole.

Neither Diane nor her children had ever been in anything so magnificent as this craft. It was the size of a small city, housing everything necessary to build a new civilization.

The Ship's Flight Control Deck was the smallest part of the massive craft. Containing an upper deck for the commander's chair, there was an observation deck capable of seating 20 and control center that had several monitoring screens and manual control area, such the need arises. The vessel operated on a central computer system and was programmed for voice command.

Three levels deep in its belly and as long as three football fields, it housed two laboratories, three large cafeterias with seating for 1500 people, fully stocked to sustain for five years. Housing compartments were scattered along all three levels. With officer quarters that offer views of the passing cosmos.

The engine room extended off the back of the hall and

contained the Stargate Chamber on its lower level.

The ship's midsection was designed as a launch station and was supplied with several smaller ships, for exploring nearby planets. It also stored the fifty robots brought along to assist John and his crew in establishing ground experiment's and setting up a base camp.

Within seconds the ship had moved from the docking bay, down the long tunnel and into alignment with the gateway. At warp speed, they moved from the center of the Earth, out beyond the gravitational pull of the planet. Concordance set for their three-month long journey, they approached the black hole and slipped thru its opening.

As the ship flew through the wormhole created by the concordances, the passengers watched in awe as they slipped thru beautiful strands of colors. Clouds of nebulae and stars could be seen as the ship moved closer and closer to its destination.

John looked over at Diane and said, "I had the strangest dream last night!"

Chapter Thirty

Left Alone

The population of Satara climaxed at 8 Billion Souls when the War with the A.I. broke out. Those that survived the earth changes, deadly viruses, and catastrophic weather, were now made to witness a civilization on the brink of extinction. With a population of less than 500 million, Men outnumbered their female counterparts by 1 to 1000, with the odds of those women being able to reproduce to even less 1/1 millionth of a chance.

Once the Elite that governed the planet had evacuated, those left behind were suddenly made aware of all that had taken place, while they were under the control of the powerful organization.

The Wars that had now taken the lives of billions of loved ones, friends and families, had been going on for generations. Producing war machines, fathom, diseases and mass hysteria, feeding the beast known as A.I. How their technologies kept the energy of the people at a low vibration, giving "them" complete control of their lives.

All electrical grids were starting to shut down. Satellites falling from the skies above, shutting down communications and throwing the World Wide Web offline.

With no real authority, those that were employed by the Military, along with those able among the men and woman that survived and took control of what was left of the City's throughout Satara. The A.I. may have won the war, but the battle continued, as there were those willing to fight back for their planet, their way of living and their right to exist.

A group of men positioned all across the globe were given orders to carry out the annihilation of the A.I., these men referred to themselves as The Illuminated ones.

Made in the USA
Columbia, SC
06 October 2023